EXIT
PATH

: stories :

by

Charlotte Cooper

ISBN: 978-0-984-697793

First Edition.

DEDICATION:

I dedicate this book to:

Ann Simone Cooper, Austin Cooper,
Robin Cooper, John Donovan,
Jny Wittker and all those who have been
in Nazi concentration camps.

AUTHOR'S NOTE:

All the stories herein are fiction. Any resemblance to any person, living or dead, is purely accidental.

Charlotte Cooper

TABLE OF CONTENTS

Love, Loss & Letting Go

Wisdom & Gratitude

PREFACE

As a volunteer who sits with patients in hospitals and nursing homes writing letters or just listening to them, I often hear stories that have never been told to anyone, even their family.

My husband was in the military and as we traveled all over the country, I discovered that the elderly and the ill had many joys, regrets and; sometimes, amends to make. Some stories were very sad ones and others were quite funny, but all of them had wisdom to share.

Have you ever heard of neurotheology? When I sat with people and listened to their stories I realized that it does not matter what color skin you have, or which religion, or whether you are rich or poor, or famous or not — just as long as you have a belief. I have found that it does help to have a faith when facing difficult situations.

I also realized that the one thing everyone seeks from childhood to adult life is to be loved. Without this bonding, lives go awry. Wisdom comes with age. Perhaps one or two of these stories may leave a mark on the lives of some readers.

Charlotte Cooper

REGRETS

&

AMENDS

FRIEDA

In 1986, in Ohio, I was told one of the most tragic and funny stories I have ever heard. My friend Frieda was a new resident at the nursing home. She was very young to be in such an environment and naturally I was curious to hear her story. Here is what she told me.

I hope to leave here as soon as my neck is out of this brace. What happened is a strange turn of events.

I was married to someone for twenty-five years. He grew up in a small town and had a high school sweetheart who became pregnant by another classmate. That classmate married her. That was the story I was told, and since I did not live in that town or anywhere near it, I believed that story.

My husband died two weeks ago. It was a graveside funeral service. I was placing a rose on the coffin, which had been lowered into the freshly dug grave. Just as I was bending over to put the rose down, a young man stepped up to me. He was the spitting image of my husband. I was so surprised; I tripped and fell into the hole on top of the coffin, which injured my back and neck. All those years I believed that story, but the moment my eyes looked at that face I knew it was a big lie.

This young man used his cell phone to call 911, and I was rushed to the hospital. A few days passed, and who walked into my hospital room but that familiar face. He told me his parents moved away some years ago; however, after reading the obituary in the paper he decided to attend the funeral.

"I knew my father was so different in every way," he said. "It just seemed impossible for me to believe he was my natural birth father. Plus, I certainly did not favor my mother. It was an odd feeling that I kept to myself until I met an old friend of my mother's. She was the kind of person who would say what was on her mind. 'Oh you look exactly like so and so,' she would say."

Well, I had to satisfy my curiosity and see for myself. Unfortunately, it was a closed casket and graveside service. Perhaps you have a photo I can look at?" I said that I'd give him all the photos I had and to leave his address so that they could be mailed to him. With a thank you he left.

Still humiliated and angry over how I was deceived for twenty-five years, I threw things at the wall. The doctor medicated me, and after one week in the hospital I was sent to this nursing home in a straightjacket. A sign was put on my door: "No visitors allowed."

Eventually, I was released from the hospital. The young man, Richard Wells, received the photos I sent him. Then, one day I received a phone call from him.

"Frieda, I want to know more about my father," he told me. "Please, please help me."

I couldn't deny Richard and invited him to visit. The day Richard arrived I placed more family photos on the table, showing him grandparents he had never known and photos from when his father was growing up. Richard was in tears as we talked and compared family traits. I think it gave Richard closure and it gave me the feeling that my husband was living on in him.

We met once a month at first and then our visits became weekly ones. We grew closer with a gentle kind of love that continued through the years, easing any bitterness either of us might have held.

"You are the first person I have told this story to!" Frieda exclaimed. "Isn't it crazy the tricks life can play on us?

I had to agree with Frieda. I reassured her that I thought she had done the right thing. Frieda left the nursing home but had to return for therapy treatments. We had many long talks about how happy she was that fate had allowed her to find peace with her beloved husband.

JOE & LOUIS

This story was told to me by an attorney who came from West Texas, who never told me his real name.

Four teenage boys, between the ages of seventeen and eighteen, were on Spring break from the high school from which they would soon graduate.

The United States had just entered WWII, and these boys knew that for them it was either the adventure of war or working in the cotton fields. All four buddies decided to enlist rather than wait to be drafted. This weekend would be their last to have some fun.

Joe, Tom, Jerry and Fred set out for a drive in an old pick-up truck that was on Tom's family farm. To make the trip more exciting they decided to capture some armadillos and put them into cartons.

Now, armadillos are slow-moving creatures and roam the roads in western Texas, but they do have claws that are dangerous if one is not careful. Most folks just leave them be, because sooner or later they will become road kill on the highways.

The boys captured two creatures of medium size and placed each one into their own carton with string tied around to keep them closed. Joe, with his red hair blowing in the West Texas wind, said he would sit in the back of the truck and toss the boxes when given the signal.

Tom drove through a part of the country where mostly black people lived. It was dusk and almost nightfall without a bright moon that evening, and it seemed the ideal time for some fun.

The signal was given to Joe to toss one carton and after a short distance given another signal to toss the other one. Being curious and with high hopes of returning with something worthwhile, black kids of all sizes ran out onto the road to pick up the boxes.

The first box was opened and the creature startled the young kids, so they just let it go. The second box was opened that held a somewhat larger armadillo that was feistier. These boys thought they could tease it out with a stick, but when one boy bent over to get a better look at it, the armadillo's claw ripped his face.

The four boys knew the kids would look inside, but never gave a thought to what those armadillos would do. The boys heard the screams, and sped away never to return to that part of town again. However, Joe's red hair was not forgotten by one boy who screamed bloody murder with pain.

The boy, dripping in blood, walked into his house. His father was drunk and laughed at him. His mother dragged him into the kitchen to clean up the mess. With no car and no money, it was impossible to go to the hospital thirty-five miles away. Momma did the best she could to stop the bleeding and to bandage the wound. Having injuries and accidents was not a new or scary thing to most black folks in that part of the country, and they coped the best way they could.

At their graduation party, the four boys agreed never to mention that fateful night to anyone. Each one knew, whether you were black or white, that the police would punish them for such a terrible prank on innocent boys.

The four buddies went into the Army and stayed together through training camp until they were given tests that would determine their talents. Tom was a good driver, who in time drove an ambulance. Joe, who had an artistic bent, worked in the kitchens here and in France. Jerry and Fred were sent to the rifle field, since they were good shooters. Both of these boys were killed in action in Italy.

Tom met a French girl, who was a nurse. She came to the U.S. at the end of the war and they married. They moved to Dallas, and Tom drove a truck for a living.

Joe stayed in the small West Texas town and worked on the family farm. He decided to use the GI Bill and go to barber school. The following year, he moved to the next town where there was a larger population and opened his shop. His parents hired help to work the farm, and they were happy to see him branch out on his own. Joe was friendly to everyone. The love of his life in high school married someone else during those war years and it broke his heart, so he never married.

It was during the late 1950s and early 1960s when the schools were integrated in West Texas. HUD had built low rental houses that changed many areas. Black people, especially, started to better their situation — many stayed in school and some went on to college or trade schools.

One day a tall black man, with a scar on his face from his temple down to his chin, walked into Joe's barbershop looking for work. His name was Louie. He said he had finished barber school and specialized in cutting black men's hair. Joe needed the help and hire him on the spot. It was a shrewd decision since many blacks were getting jobs at the new chicken hatchery just out of town.

Louie proved to be an excellent companion in the shop, always neat and friendly with all the customers. Joe and Louie had a good business through the years. It was around 1975 when Joe suffered a stroke that paralyzed him on one side. Unable to work anymore, he asked Louie if he wanted to purchase the shop and all the equipment at a very reasonable price. Louie jumped at the offer.

Joe's parents had died and his only brother was killed during the war in the Pacific. The farm was sold after the death of his parents. Joe lived in a small house close to his shop and thought life was good to him. He was happy with his work and struck gold when Louie worked for him. Business had never been so good. Louie not only managed the shop, but also checked on Joe every day before going to work, and in the evenings.

There were times when Joe thought about that prank the four buddies pulled, but never talked about, and which no one knew the outcome of that night. The scream haunted Joe's memory and he felt responsible because it was he alone who had tossed those boxes.

One day Joe asked Louie how he got the scars on his face. Louie told him about the white boys out for a night of fun with some armadillos. Joe started to cry when he heard the story, but quickly covered it with a coughing spell.

When Joe came home from the war, he was twenty-three years old and starting to lose his hair, just like his father who was bald at an early age. That flame of red hair on his dome was out, and what was left had started to turn grey. Therefore, when Louie met Joe he never imagined he was that white boy with the red hair who had tossed that fated box. Their friendship was strong, but not strong enough to be told the truth.

Joe passed away one night. It was Louis who arranged a military funeral. There was a crowd of local people and many from the small town where Joe grew up. Fred, the last living of the four buddies, came from Dallas to say goodbye to an old friend and gave a final salute to a fellow soldier.

After the bugler played "Taps," Louie waved for all to stay seated because he wanted to read something. It was the story of his friendship with Joe. There was not a dry eye in the crowd and when they left each one gave Louie a hug and thanked him for his loyalty to his friend.

It was a week later, when Louie and his wife were watching TV, when someone came to their door. He introduced himself as Joe's attorney. The attorney pulled out papers from a briefcase saying, "You are one lucky man." Joe had bequeathed all the money from the farm and the mineral rights, which meant oil money, someday. Louie signed those papers.

The attorney said he was not finished and pulled out more papers to be signed. This was for full ownership of the shop with all the equipment canceling the remaining debt, plus all the money that Joe had saved through the years. Louie and his wife were in total shock and disbelief that anyone would be so generous. They cried out of joy and out of friendship. The attorney closed his briefcase. They shook hands and said good night.

The attorney walked down the street to his car shaking his head. He wondered why Joe had made him promise not to tell what he had confided in him when he drew up the papers — that Joe had been the one responsible for Louie's disfigurement. As far as I know, the secret that haunted Joe to his grave was never revealed to anyone other than his attorney — and myself.

Some secrets are better left untold. Making silent restitution for a wrong can sometimes be a better balm than causing shock or hurt to someone we love. The important thing is to make amends.
I wonder if Louie ever guessed that Joe was the cause of his childhood accident or that his presence in Joe's life made all the difference.

ARNE

Life is often full of unexpected twists and turns. In 1970 Arne Swendson, who was a hospice patient, related this story of love, loss and reunion to me.

It was December 1929, several weeks after the New York stock market crashed. It was a depressing time for all who worked in New York City. Christopher and Jude had been friends and neighbors, even having graduated college together. They were fortunate to have jobs with insurance firms and wanted to celebrate.

Christopher invited Jude to his home for a spaghetti dinner. Carol, Christopher's wife, served a lovely meal. She was pleased to see Jude again since they did not meet that often. The young men went into the living room to chat over old times. On the table next to the sofa was a photograph of a pretty girl. Jude asked who the girl was, and Chris said, "It's my sister-in-law, Linda." Chris said he would arrange a blind date for him. Jude said, "I would appreciate knowing a little about Linda first." Jude was not too fond of Carol, who was proper but not very friendly or jovial. If the sister was the same, he would not be interested.

Chris said, "I'll tell you what I know about the sisters. Both girls were orphans. At ages four and two, their mother died having a third baby. The father was from Sweden, the mother was from Danzig, Germany. Even before WWII, many people were immigrating to the United States for a better life. Carol's and Linda's parents met on the ship coming to the States. I guess it was love the moment they met because they married soon after and settled in the city.

It was after the mother died, when the father, Arne Swendson, decided to place the girls in a state orphanage. The girls stayed there until ages fourteen and sixteen, when a minister and his wife adopted them. They never had any contact by letter or in person from their father, nor did they have photos of their parents. There was just a big void when it came to their past history. They enjoyed life in the minister's household and continued their education. Both worked in the church records department, and they were always there serving meals at the different functions. It was a good life.

Carol and I met at one of the church dinners. Carol was twenty years old when we married. Linda stayed with the minister and his wife to work in the church office and continue her education. Jude, I can assure you that Linda is a sweet girl and very outgoing. What I truly like about the sisters is that they never expect much, and they were appreciative for the smallest token bestowed upon them."

It was about two years after Chris had given this background about the two sisters when Jude and Linda were married. Jude and Chris decided to purchase a family house together in the Yonkers area of New York. Jude and Linda had a son, and Chris and Carol had a girl. They made a harmonious foursome, playing bridge, and having a family dinner together on Saturday nights. All was well in spite of the Depression years that affected so many. However, the girls always wondered about their real parents. It wasn't until years later that they were to learn about their history or that it was a letter from their mother that eventually made it possible for the following events to unfold.

When their parents Arne and Anna Swendson came to America, life was not easy, but they were not lazy and managed to find a small apartment on the west side in downtown Manhattan. Arne found work in a shirt factory cutting patterns. It was a steady job.

Anna did bookkeeping for a small restaurant that was located down the street. They had dreams of a better life one day. Holding onto that dream became an obsession. They purchased only what they needed, to the point that being frugal took the joy out of living.

When Anna died, Arne did not accept his loneliness. After the funeral notices were mailed to families in Europe, Arne fell into a depression. He knew that he could not care for the babies he loved so dearly. One day he took the girls to an orphanage and stood at the door, undecided if he should press the doorbell. With tears running down his cheeks, he went ahead and pressed the bell.

It was his co-workers at the factory who took pity upon Arne and brought him back to his old self. He studied for his citizenship, which was granted. Mr. Schwartz, the owner of the shirt factory, pulled Arne aside for a man-to-man chat. He told Arne, "You are too intelligent to stay here cutting patterns. I am going to introduce you to a friend of mine." A meeting was arranged and, to Arne's surprise, this friend worked for the FBI.

Arne was gifted in that he knew Russian, Polish, German and Swedish. He had a well-rounded education in his native land. Arne went for an interview in Washington, D.C. and was hired as a translator. Arne said goodbye to all his co-workers and thanked Mr. Schwartz for changing his life. The fellow workers had a going away party and wished him good luck.

Germany was changing in so many ways at that time. Many people who could afford to leave were traveling to other countries and the U.S. government wanted to know more about what was happening. The FBI knew Arne's background and he was asked if he would like to visit his family, but most of all to visit the family of his deceased wife. Arne agreed, and all the papers were in order for a friendly visit to both countries. He was to travel around Germany as a tourist, visit his wife's family in Danzig, and then visit his own parents in Sweden. He was instructed not to take notes or contact anyone in Washington D.C. during his travels.

He had never met his deceased wife's family, although he had heard stories from Anna how hard her parents worked in a gristmill, preparing and shipping the grain. When he arrived in Danzig, the household was not at all like the picture Anna had painted in Arne's mind. This was obviously a very wealthy family — but one with a mysterious, dark past. Arne had a luscious, luxurious meal and stayed several hours in their beautiful home, talking about his work in the shirt factory and how happy he had been with Anna. Never did Arne mention his position in the FBI. To them, he was just another poor factory worker who had saved his money for this trip.

It was during that dinner that he learned that his wife had written a letter to the family about their life, the birth of two girls, plus a third baby soon to be born. Without this letter, they would never have known about Carol and Linda or thought to ask about the children. The last mail to reach them was the note Arne had sent them with the funeral notice of Anna's death. The family members were not pleased to learn that he had put the girls in an orphanage. They wanted to have photos and not to lose contact with the girls again.

Arne wanted to visit the gristmill that Anna had spoken about. Her family very quickly refused, saying they had sold that business and now worked for the German government. Arne asked if they could show him the old port city of Danzig and they replied, "We are not permitted to enter there without a special pass." One hesitation and refusal after another caught Arne by surprise. The family told him, "It would be safe to see Germany if you took a tour." The word 'safe' gave Arne goose bumps. He thanked them for their gracious hospitality. He promised to locate the girls and have them correspond.

Arne's travels around Germany proved that there were many changes. Residents could only purchase a limited amount of food, the first signs of rationing to be imposed. The Hitler Youth Groups were wearing uniforms and marching around Berlin. They were being trained for a future army. In the area outside the city there were many people being transported by train. Yes! Something was on the mind of that leader, Hitler. Arne made no notes, but kept it all in his head for his future reports.

He traveled to Sweden to visit his parents and sisters. His mother was delighted to see him after all those years of having a vacant spot in her heart. The sisters kissed and hugged him, but the father, now in his 80s, was still the disciplinarian. Kurt Swendson was a professor of history and accustomed to giving orders to students. He expected too much from Arne when he was young, and there was always an undercurrent of friction between the two since Arne was his only son. This was the main reason Arne left home after college.

Life was pretty much the same for the family after the father retired. Sweden in general looked the same. Arne visited some old friends and had a pleasant one-week visit. The family wanted to learn more about his daughters and prayed that they had a good life. His mother said, "We would love to see them, but we understand why you gave them up.

"However, they are not to travel to Europe," his father insisted. "That madman, Hitler, is up to something." Arne said his goodbyes. He traveled back to America on the ship "Europa." It was 1934 when the ship left Europe. On board Arne met many German Jews who left everything behind just to live in another country. They were allowed only a small amount of money when they left Germany.

Arne reported back to Washington D.C. and gave his impressions of his travels, and it was shortly after this visit that all mail from Germany was censored. Arne remained as a translator and was often selected for special duty. To fulfill his promises to both families, he was determined to locate his daughters. He also wanted to satisfy himself that he had made the proper decision years ago, a decision that haunted him with nightmares and depression. Those sweet babies just had to have a good life. It was time Arne found out.

It had been many years ago when Arne had pressed the same doorbell to the orphanage to say goodbye to his two small girls. Now he was back, and he wanted information as to their whereabouts. After his identity was confirmed, the name of a local minister was given. After several phone calls, an appointment was made to meet with the minister and his wife.

Arne assured them he meant no harm, but was anxious to see the girls. He explained his early hardships, but that now he was employed by the government. He wanted the girls to know their families in Europe and that of his deceased wife.

It was a joyous event for the girls to see their father and to share their stories into the wee hours of the morning. Carol and Linda were grateful to the minister and his wife, but it meant so much more to know they had a real family. The girls now understood their father's reason for giving them up and nothing more was said. They were overjoyed to have a completed story.

One sunny September day, the news came over the radio that Hitler had invaded Poland. Everything that Arne had seen and heard became true and the horrors of war changed many lives. Arne found out that his wife's family in Danzig was involved in manufacturing war supplies. The family was killed during one of the bombings and their factories were destroyed.

In the late 1950s, Carol and Linda visited their family in Sweden. The grandparents had died, but they were delighted to know their cousins, and they started a family tree. They were not able to visit East Germany, but from what they heard it was for the best.

The visit changed the sisters' lives forever. Shortly after meeting their father, Linda wrote this poem:

No more lonely hours of the night.
Dear father you have lifted up my heart,
I no longer hide under a veil of dark,
Dear father you have filled me with joy,
love and delight.

Their father visited often and showered the grandchildren with love and gifts. There was finally closure to their great mystery, thanks to their mother's letter and the United States Government, who made their father a spy.

Arne's story reminds me that the decisions we make when we are young often have long-lasting consequences and yet sometimes what seems like the worst of situations, may turn out for the best.

CHRISTABELLA

They say that truth is stranger than fiction. This story was told to me by Louise, a ninety-two-year-old woman who was in the hospital for surgery. She had a daughter that visited her two times each day. The daughter was very pretty, and pleasant enough, but seemed distraught. One night they argued — about her name. I thought this was a strange thing to have words over.

The daughter said, "All my friends think my name is so beautiful, and different; and yet you never once called me by my name. It is always 'Honey,' 'Dearie' or' Sweetie,' and Daddy did the same thing. Now I want to know why you selected the name. What is wrong with Christabella? Please, once and for all, tell me! Daddy is dead, and now you are the only one left to ask."

For the next three days the daughter continued with the same question. Finally I asked Louise, "What on earth is the mystery about her name?"

Louise sighed and told me the deep dark secret that had weighed heavily on her heart for many years.

It was during the Great Depression years. My husband, Johnnie, said we should rent out the extra room in our house. The brownstone apartment we were renting had a perfect floor plan to accommodate a renter. The room was somewhat isolated from our living quarters. In order to use the bathroom, one would have to enter through a hallway, and at the other end of the hallway was our kitchen door, which had a lock. Many neighbors who had this floor plan were renting out this extra bedroom or study during these bad times. I did not think it was wise to have a man; therefore we advertised for a woman who was employed, who did not require the use of a kitchen, but only the bathroom.

It was not long after this ad was placed that a young woman rang my doorbell. She had an excellent position that would require some traveling; therefore she did not require a large apartment. Miss Christabella Giovanni was a dark-haired, attractive young lady. It did not take me long for to decide to rent to her. I gave her a key to the front door and one to her room. The Saturday she moved in was the first time my husband met her.

I was busy taking care of our first born, a boy, who had a bad cough and was rather sickly. The cough developed into pneumonia, and he died. At that time all the miracle drugs were not available to cure him.

One night I heard noise and talking from Miss Giovanni's room and thought it was a visitor. Then a few nights after that, the visitor was back.

In our verbal agreement about renting, there was no stipulation about visitors or noise. My husband usually returned home from the office around 5:30 p.m., but there were times when he worked late and returned around 8:30-9:00 p.m.

When the talking and what sounded like pushing against the wall continued, I grew curious. One night when my husband did not return at 5:30 p.m., I decided to sit in the living room and keep watch. I sat near the window, which had a curtain and drapery, but through a narrow space I was able to see who came into the front door. I knew Miss Giovanni was in her room; she had returned around 5:00 p.m. with some takeout food, which was her usual routine. But lo and behold, if it wasn't Johnnie who entered next, using the extra key to her room. I ran to the kitchen to see if the extra key was on the hook. It was still hanging there, which meant another one had to have been made. Again low voices, almost a mumbling — then a sudden quiet.

It was 9:00 p.m. when the door to the kitchen opened, and Johnnie walked in. I asked him how many evenings did he think the company would ask him to work late? I was annoyed trying to keep food warm for his dinner. He replied, "I can't answer that."

I thought we had a loving relationship, up until the baby got so ill; then there were some turbulent nights with little sleep. The coughing and rocking him back to sleep caused our sleep patterns to be disrupted. I was tired and unhappy after our adorable baby died. Perhaps I was not as attractive; perhaps I did not really know Johnnie. All these questions kept spinning in my mind. If he needed another woman, how could I trust him? How many others were there?

Miss Giovanni left on one of her business trips and would be gone two to four days. It was during one of those nights when Johnnie became demanding in bed. I never denied him his pleasure; but he was abusive and forceful. I blurted out, 'Too bad Miss Giovanni is not in her room; you do know I am asking her to leave as soon as she returns.'

In those days people did not get divorces. It was considered a disgrace. Women were encouraged to keep their mouths shut about their husband's infidelities.

It was almost eight weeks later when I was positive that I was pregnant. I tried to be happy about having another baby, but things were not the same as with the first pregnancy. The touching of my belly to feel the baby move, the selection of names for a boy or a girl, the sweet talk, the anticipation of a new baby were all lacking, even though Johnnie promised to be faithful.

A neighbor took me to the hospital one morning and sat with me. When the nurse came into the room she asked if we had a girl's name. I knew there could only be one choice, "Christabella," to remind Johnnie of his unfaithfulness.

The baby girl was beautiful from the first day and so easy to manage. She was lovely all through the years of growing up. But I could never bring myself to say her name, and Johnnie refused to say it. He was angry with me for that selection, which was hurtful and indicative of his unfaithfulness. We called her anything but her given name. It was 'Honey', 'Sweetie', 'Dearie', or 'Sugar' at all times. In school she had to write her given name, and all her friends called her Christabella. It was not a common name, and it did have a nice musical ring to it. It was no wonder that everyone thought it was a sweet name.

I never could bring myself to tell her this story. I beg you to do it for me; I have the strangest feeling that I will not make it through this surgery. Please do this favor for me. It will give both of us peace, and I will know that finally I did the right thing by her.

"Of course I will tell her the story," I promised Louise. "I know she will understand that she was loved."

It was a lovely morning with the sunshine filtering through the windows, but my thoughts were in a tailspin. I wondered how on earth I, a perfect stranger, could tell Christabella such a story. I felt, instinctively, that it would crush her. I had to think fast. Louise was wheeled into surgery and only a few moments passed before the door opened and the daughter said, "Good morning."

"Oh please sit down close to me, Christabella," I said. "I have something to tell you. As I promised your mother, this is the untold story about your name."

As you know, your mother is ninety-two and felt that she may not pull through this surgery; and as a result I promised to share this story with you.

Your parents married in 1936, and those Depression years were leaving their mark on just about everyone. In order to make ends meet after the expense of the burial for your baby brother, they decided to rent out a room. This was a common practice in those desperate years.

The ad was placed in the newspaper for an employed female. A lovely young lady, Christabella

Carbona, who was eighteen or nineteen years old, answered the ad. She was employed as a secretary and was also going to school in the evenings.

It seemed too good to be true, a renter, on the very same day the doctor told your mother she was pregnant with you.

Your parents took a fond liking to this young girl who had been orphaned when both parents died while emigrating from Italy to America. Upon arrival, Christabella was immediately put into a Catholic orphanage. She spent her entire childhood there and once she turned eighteen, she was given a choice to be a nun or go out into the work force. Like so many other girls in the orphanage, she was educated to work in an office. Christabella was a skilled secretary and found work for a large music publisher. She loved her job and decided to continue with her education by going to college at night.

One night, about six months later, a policeman came to the door. Christabella had been killed in a tragic car accident and they were called to identify the body. They had come to love Christabella and it just about broke your parents' hearts.

They did not have any extra money, and your mother was pregnant. Therefore they did the best *thing possible, and laid Christabella to rest in Potter's Field. They were sorry that they could not afford a stone marker, but they made a wooden cross that would suffice until they could afford one.*

When they gave you her name, they did not know the effect it would have on them. Your parents loved Christabella in the same way they have always loved you, but because of the sad accident they simply felt guilty and sad. It was because of this guilt that they could not call you by her name; it brought back memories that were just too painful.

Christabella, you were given a name out of love. It turned out to be bittersweet, but nevertheless it was love. Remember that they both adored you. That is all that matters in this world — that we know how to give and receive love.

At that moment, the doctor entered the room without a smile on his face. He did not have to say anything. We both knew that Louise had died.

Christabella kissed me goodbye and said, "I have always loved my parents and even more so now. Thank you from the bottom of my heart for solving this mystery. I will always be grateful to you!"

Sometimes the raw truth is too hurtful. I never felt any remorse about telling Christabella this fictionalized account, and never in my life did I feel better about being a storyteller at heart.

MYSTERIES

&

CONFESSIONS

BILLY JEAN

In 1960, I met Billy Jean, who was a new patient at the nursing home. She had come to receive a daily routine of physical therapy for a fall she had taken. She lived with her son and his wife and their dog, a Great Dane. It was the dog that had pushed her over, breaking several bones.

I asked her if she wanted to continue to live at the house. This is what she told me.

Until recently, the house I live in was a mystery. The place still gives me the jitters. Whenever I walk outside near the decking and hot tub, the hair on my neck and arms still bristle. If anyone thinks having ESP is a blessing they should think again, because when there is something wrong you can't sleep and all those strange feelings keep you in a state of anxiety.

I was determined to find out if my ESP was telling me if something strange happened there or if it was my imagination. My son told me to mind my own business, but I could not help myself. One day I noticed an elderly neighbor, Mrs. Wilson, and I asked her about the previous owners. Mrs. Wilson was relieved to finally give confide her story. "I believe there was a murder," she said. "But the police had no proof, and it was written up as an accident."

"The owners who purchased the house before your son did a lot of remodeling and repairs," she continued. "They added a large family room, the deck outside for a hot tub, changed the staircase to the basement and several other things. The husband, Larry Woodard, was an executive for a firm here and traveled out of state, so he was often gone for several days at a time. The wife, Emily Woodard, was a pretty young nurse who worked at the local hospital. She was known to help people and had a young fellow call on her when Larry was gone on business."

Mrs. Wilson did not want me to think she was a nosey person. But, as she said, because the two houses were close together and she sat outside, either on the front or back porch, she could see who was coming and going.

"It's possible," Mrs. Wilson said, "that Emily was helping the young fellow or more likely he was her lover. I never liked the looks of that boy. At first he was so shabbily dressed, and then he was wearing new shoes and expensive clothes. I think the husband was so busy with his work, and he believed Emily was kind-hearted in helping another person as she had in the past. One day she asked me to take her mail and hold it for her because Larry might not be home the same day. This was not too unusual and I was happy to help her."

Mrs. Wilson continued. "The next few days, still no Emily. I did notice her car in the driveway very early one morning. Then the husband came home in a taxi that afternoon. And before you could blink an eye, the police were all over the place. Of course, Larry had the excuse and proof of flying in from out of town. The young fellow gave his story and informed the police at the beach and the local police here. The police questioned the young boy, but because of his innocent manner and his hysterical mood, he came across as a small, ashen, miserable, sad young kid who was lost without his dear friend. That being said, he did not fool me with his fits of weeping. I think he was driven by lust and saw money every time he was with Emily, but I kept my thoughts to myself. After all what proof did I have?"

"The young kid told the police, 'We were at the beach late one night when the lifeguard was off duty. Emily loved to ride the waves. She was out some distance and then simply was gone'. The kid said he was not a good swimmer and the beach was deserted.

There was no one he could ask for help. So he went to the police, gave his story and drove Emily's car home. I remember that morning I had heard some noise, but it was dark outside and I was not interested in getting out of bed to check it out. Emily's husband went back to the beach and made inquiries, but it was always a dead-end trail. Emily's mother came to stay in the house with Larry. She was so distraught it was impossible to converse with her. The young kid was found not guilty, and there was no body, so the case was written up as an accident."

I told Mrs. Wilson that every time I walked on that deck I knew something was amiss and terribly wrong. Later, I was so glad that my son decided to take out the hot tub and put down new decking.

The workmen came to remove the hot tub and the old decking. They said they would be back to replace the decking as soon as they had the lumber. After they left, I took a shovel and started to dig. After two hours of laborious work, I uncovered a sheet with what looked like a body of bones. When my son came home from work, he called the police. I called Mrs. Wilson and announced, "The case of the mystery is solved." She was happy to hear that her instincts had been correct, too.

The police asked me a ton of questions. They thought it was strange that after ten years I knew where to dig up those bones. I told them, "That young kid brought the body back and buried it right under your noses. Since Emily was a tiny person, it was probably easy to bury her body under the deck."

Finally, I confessed to the police about my ESP. The police said, 'We could use you when we have a difficult case — are you interested?' I was told to go to Stanford University and be tested, but I never did. Imagine, in my old age finding employment doing what comes naturally!"

People who have personally experienced psychic phenomena know that there are many things in life that simply cannot be explained. The story Billy Jean told me is an example of how belief in one's intuition can sometimes provide the answers to those mysteries.

DOCTOR HENDERSON

The following story was told to me by a woman on her deathbed. She had grown up in an affluent neighborhood in a beach community and lived a very privileged life.

Dr. Henderson, a neurology surgeon, had three daughters and a pretty wife. The girls, Emily, Edna, and Etta were teenagers, all excellent students and were involved in sports at the local high school. His wife kept very busy with volunteer work and several clubs.

Dr. Henderson had a lovely, vivacious nurse in his office, with whom he had been having an affair for some years. The nurse, with her charming way and flights of fancy and make believe, won the girls over without suspicions. She always invited the girls to join her in her swimming pool on the weekends. The nurse lived within a reasonable walking distance, and it was not unusual to see the girls laughing and joking and entering through the iron gates to her backyard for a swim on weekends. The girls loved to swim, but as they got older they were not so gullible and could see through the nurse's scheming ways to have their father all for herself.

It was a hot summer evening, almost dusk, when the girls entered through the back gate, singing and laughing. But this evening was different, because the girls never went swimming when it was dark. Secondly, they knew that the nurse had a drinking problem and that she was often inebriated by dinnertime. The girls enticed the nurse to come out and join in the fun. They acted more jovial, splashing around and singing. The nurse came out of the house holding a drink in one hand and the bottle in the other.

She was very drunk. The girls helped her into the pool and rested her on the inflated float mattress and placed the drink in her hand. They continued to laugh and joke and have a good time. When the sky turned dark, the three girls gathered around her. Suddenly, they flipped the float over and held the nurse's head down. When all life seemed to cease, the float was tipped upward and the nurse's body was ever so serenely placed on top with the glass in her hand. The girls splashed and giggled as they continued to sing pop songs for quite some time.

The body looked so natural. As the girls got out of the pool, they put the beach towels around their bodies and waved good-bye, yelling, "Thank you for the fun time!" Then, in the dark, they gave the float a little push so that the body would again tip over.

"See you next week," they shouted and left closing the iron gate behind them. They walked home singing and greeted their mother with kisses. When Dr Henderson entered the house he was given the usual hugs. It had been a busy day and he was ready to eat his late dinner when the phone rang. The girls were ready to jump out of their skins and thought, 'not this soon.' But it was just a routine call.

On Monday morning, when the nurse did not show up for work and the waiting room was crowded with patients, Dr. Henderson called a neighbor to check in on the nurse. The neighbor called Dr. Henderson back with some sad news, and then the police called. Dr. Henderson identified the body, and the police came to the house to question the girls. All three girls told about the good time they'd had that evening and the fact that the nurse had been drinking — how much they did not know. Their stories were convincing and each one was sobbing up a storm of tears. The case was written up as an accident due to drinking.

The three girls went on to become doctors of psychiatry at a leading medical school. They lived separate lives and although each one had lovers through the years, they never married. They never spoke about the incident.

The youngest sister, Etta, made this confession to me just before she died. She could not carry that burden to her grave as the two older sisters did. As far as I know, I am the only one who has ever heard this story.

HERBIE

This story was related to me by a man in Dallas, Texas. Please note that it contains what some may consider X-rated information.

Herbie and his wife, Rose, shared a room at a nursing home for close to a year. They seemed amiable towards each other, but also towards all the others in the home.

Everyone thought Herbie would leave this world first, but instead his wife died before he did. He gave away her clothes and was most generous with her costume jewelry. There was one thing Herbie refused to open, a small hard suitcase with a combination lock on it. Herbie instructed the staff that it was for his attorney friend, Max Miller, and on top of the suitcase he taped Max's business card.

One day a letter arrived from the attorney's firm stating that Max Miller had died. Herbie read that letter over and over and cursed and cursed. Everyone could hear and wondered what the big deal was about. Those who knew about the suitcase thought that Herbie could give the suitcase to the firm and distribute the contents through his Will. Nobody could understand his uproar and anger. He caused such a disturbance that he had to be sedated. Folks thought perhaps that his attorney's passing had brought up the grief over his wife's death.

In time, Herbie became more reasonable and snapped back to his old friendly ways. His doctor was a handsome young fellow who recently married, but he never smiled or seemed happy. Herbie could not resist being inquisitive, thinking it must be the doctor's long hours or just maybe that his sex life was off base. Each time the questions were put to the doctor, the doctor simply shrugged his shoulders. He never gave a direct answer to please Herbie.

After Herbie had another heart attack, the doctor stayed close by. It was while the doctor made his rounds to see other patients in the home that Herbie asked for a paper and pen. Herbie wrote down the numbers to the combination lock for the famous suitcase. He also wrote a little note stating, "You need to have some fun in your life."

When the doctor returned, Herbie gave him the note. The doctor looked surprised, and his curiosity was aroused to the point he could not contain himself. The young man reached for the famous suitcase and placed it on the bed alongside Herbie. The combination locked popped it open, and with little effort Herbie pushed the lid up. The doctor's face turned as red as a fox's rear end in berry time. He was in shock and took a seat.

Herbie patted his hand and told him the facts about the contents. "Shortly after I was married to a most beautiful, intelligent girl, we both became very depressed over our sex life. I could not please her. I thought I was normal in every way and had no trouble with other girls in my past, so I could not understand what was wrong now. One day I ran into my old friend, Max, who was an attorney. Surely he, who was confronted with all the strange problems in people's lives, could help me.

I related my problem and he suggested I try a prosthesis. He gave me an address where one could be made. The embarrassing situation of having one's penis measured was overwhelming, but I was determined to fix this sexual problem.

The day I picked up this extended projectile, along with a bottle of champagne and a bouquet of roses, I was jubilant. I told my wife I had a special surprise for her. That night I showed her what was made to order and hoped it would thrill her beyond her wildest dreams. The new attachment was comfortable for me, but it did nothing for my Ice Queen. We tried this method several more times. Desperate to please her, I kept having new designs made, though I was the only one who enjoyed them.

Before your eyes are all my efforts to have a happy marriage and an exciting sex life. My wife and I joked about my suitcase filled with boy's toys, and whenever we wanted to have a roll in the hay, she would select one.

I had informed Max that I was going to will this box of toys to him so that he could have fun in this old age but; alas, he left me holding the bag. Now doctor, you look like you need some fun in your life. Please take them home."

The young doctor, still greatly embarrassed, picked up the case and shook his head in amazement. Lost for words he mumbled, "Thank you, Herbie, I'm sure my wife will find them . . . interesting."

This may be the raciest story I have ever heard in all my years of listening to patients. It did not shock me, though. People often have more interesting sex lives in their old age than they did when they were young. There are definitely some benefits to growing older!

ALEXANDRIA

Sometimes things are not exactly what they seem. This somewhat shocking story was told to me by a retirement home resident who was an eyewitness to the events.

It was a sultry Southern night in 1985. Dinner was over, and most of the residents in the retirement home were in the game room watching a video. As usual, the volume was turned up loud for those that were hard of hearing. As the sun set on the cotton fields that stretched as far as the eye could see, Alexandria Leon played solitaire in her private room. She paused to type a letter, which she folded carefully and placed in an envelope. She hand addressed it to a post office box back east and then turned on the evening news.

Alexandria appeared to be in her late sixties, although no one really knew for sure. She was of medium height, with a strong box-type body with narrow hips. Her aquiline profile was neither feminine nor masculine. She seemed to be quite wealthy. Her exquisite clothes were ordered from the most expensive catalogs. She was always perfectly dressed in frilly robes or blouses with lots of lace, and always wore pants. Her shoes were for comfort, her nails were painted and her hair was coiffed each week by a local beautician.

Despite her elegant demeanor, Alexandria remained a strange enigma. There was some aura about her that didn't ring true, but the other residents couldn't quite put their finger on it. The mail she received always had the same return address as the letters she mailed. She did not request a telephone in her room, as there were no calls made and none expected. She was a true loner and kept to herself, except for meals in the dining room, where she made small talk but seldom revealed anything about her past. Since coming to the retirement home, she had never had a single visitor.

But this night was different. The receptionist was pleased to note a stretch limousine pulling up to the front door. Four sharply dressed men got out and came up to the desk and very politely asked for Alexandria. She gave them the room number, remembering how delighted she was that Alexandria had people coming to see her, and such nice people at that.

When the men entered the room, Alexandria turned around slowly, looking them up and down. She crossed her arms and sat back in her chair.

"What do you want?" she asked them.

"It took five years," one of them answered. "But Joe finally found you."

Alexandria gave a hesitant laugh. "I'm just an old lady. I don't know anyone named Joe. What do you want with me?"

The four men moved closer, surrounding Alexandria. One of them turned up the volume on the television.

"Drop the act, Alex," another of the men retorted. "Did you really think you could snitch and send three guys to the chair and get away with it?" One of the men leaned closer to Alexandria.

"There's a contract on you, Alex. Godfather's orders."

"You're crazy!" Alexandria shouted. "Get out of my room!"

But no one heard Alexandria. No one heard the gun with the silencer go off, or see the men, who escaped through the window and sped off in the limo. An hour later, when the video was over, the residents made their way back to their rooms and prepared to go to bed. Someone noticed that Alexandria's television was still blaring. It was past the 10 p.m. curfew and an aide was summoned to come turn it off.

There was a blood-curdling scream. The aide, hysterical, ran out of the room and barely managed to dial 911. When the ambulance and the police arrived, they stretched a yellow tape over the door to the bloody crime scene. A wave of fear and questioning swept through the nursing home. The residents filled the hallways trying to get a look at all the commotion.

"Who would want to murder an old lady?" they wondered. The Chief of Police summoned Dr. Noonan, Alexandria's private physician, who arrived to sign the death certificate, followed by reporters from the local television station. The next to show up were the FBI and the CIA. They cautioned everyone that this was now a Federal case and that all information was to be kept under wraps until further notice.

It wasn't until years later that the real story came to light.

First of all, Alexandria (or Alex) was not a she, but a he. Once a hit man for the mob, Alex was desperate to break ties with them. He had uncovered one of the biggest drug cartels in history and the scandal involved U.S. allies, important politicians, graft and payoffs. Alex was also a witness to a murder of a politician and his testimony sent three persons to the electric chair.

The only way Alex could leave the mob was to be given a new identity under the witness protection code. He decided to change his gender and go to a small town and live in a nursing home. If this arrangement proved to be a good cover, in a few years Alex would leave the home for good and live with an older sister outside the U.S. But Alex's conscience bothered him. He had a brother who was a priest. It was to him that he wrote each week, but he did not live to mail his last letter.

The newspaper the next day read: 'Alexandria DeLeon was born in France and married four times. The FBI is investigating what they believe is a crime of revenge.' And that, to my knowledge, was the last official mention of Alexandria (Alex) DeLeon.

SUZIE

We've all encountered messy people, but this story is a "shoe-in" for one of the most bizarre stories I have ever heard.

Jolly, jolly Suzie sat in her wheelchair eating her mid-day snack. I looked into the room and asked, "Is there anything you need?"

"No," was the quick response.

I said, "You will not be here very long. Your leg is healing quickly."

"Would you like to know how I broke it?"

"Sure, I love to listen to the stories folks tell me." I took a seat and Jolly Suzie, as everyone called her, started to reveal the facts.

I married a slob; of course I did not know that before we married. One day the mask fell off and there I was cleaning and washing, and picking up after my messy husband for fifty years. It was not in me to change a person. Change has to come from within a person, not from someone else. After a year of visits to a psychologist, who thought that I was a clean freak and that I was the one with the problem — I decided to make a change.

Every night I was worn to a frazzle, an old lump of protoplasm. Imagine this: every time it rained or snowed my husband would take his wet shoes off and place them on a step going into the basement. At the end of winter, there could be a dozen pairs of shoes, boots, and slippers sitting on those steps. It was destiny that sooner or later an accident would occur.

After fifty years of picking up after someone who could never put his clothes in the closet or pick up his shoes, or carry dirty laundry into the laundry room, I decided to just leave things where he dropped them.

New Year's Day, as he was trying to locate boots left on the steps, he misjudged a shoe for a step, and down the basement stairs he flew. He was like a cockroach on its back with all legs flopping around in mid-air. Then the flutter stopped.

All though the years of living in the same old house, I was cautious and carried a flashlight when going down the basement stairs. This accident did not give me the opportunity to find my flashlight. It was all I could do to make my path with a sure footing until I reached the bottom. He had no pulse and probably a broken neck, a nice quick way to go if one has to depart.

It was necessary to make my climb up the shoe summit; it always reminded me of mountain climbing because the handrail was never installed. I dialed 911, and the body was taken up the stairs without any trouble because I gave those fellows a bag to put all the shoes, boots, and slippers inside.

All the details dealing with the death caused from an accident were investigated and, to my amazement, this went as smooth as cream. One insurance inspector just looked around his bedroom and shook his head.

If I had continued to be the maid, this may not have happened, but everyone has limits. Then too, if the house had been spotless as in the past, I could have been accused of pushing him to his death. So there you have it — in honor of my husband, I was a slob for one year, too.

I took my time cleaning out his messy room and boxing clothes for the thrift shop. All was going so well until I stepped on a wad of chewing gum. The gum was so sticky that once it adhered to my laced shoe, I could not kick the shoe off. I lost my balance and stumbled, breaking my leg in two places.

Now, here I sit, when I had plans to travel, visit old friends, and have some freedom from cleaning house. The moral to my story is . . . always have a flashlight handy.

The psychologist was correct — Suzie was a bit of a clean freak — but turning into a slob was obviously not the answer either. No matter what the situation is in life, it is always best to try to find a happy medium.

DRAMA

&

DESTINY

MARIA

Maria was a lovely person both inside and out. She was an unusual beauty even at the age of seventy. She had worked all her life as a physician serving poor populations in Southern California and later became a noted philanthropist. When I met Maria, she was recovering from surgery for stomach cancer.

Maria grew up in California, a Mexican beauty who looked more Asian than Mexican. Her skin was like a white china plate surrounded with black hair, and dark, enticing eyes that would dance when she spoke to someone.

In 1939 her parents traveled from Mexico to California to work in the vegetable fields under the supervision of a local farmer, Mr. Blackly. The Blacklys were kind people and had a small house on the property where her parents, Pedro and Arrayo, could make a home. Pedro was learning English. It wasn't long before Mr. Blackly trusted Pedro to put him in charge of the other farm help. Arrayo worked in the house for Mrs. Blackly and helped cook meals for the workers.

Arrayo became pregnant but continued to work. Mrs. Blackly was delighted since she never could have children and regarded this event as a blessing in their lives as well as Pedro's and Arrayo's. The two ladies busied themselves making baby clothes and decorating both houses for the newcomer.

One evening after dinner, Arrayo did not feel well — it was time for that special event. Mrs. Blackly drove Pedro and Arrayo to the local hospital. Within a few hours a beautiful baby girl was born, and she was named Maria. When Maria was about two months old and her features were more distinct, she certainly did not look like a Mexican baby. Maria looked distinctly Asian; with white skin, black hair, and almond-shaped eyes.

Pedro looked astonished and told the Blacklys a story that was often repeated in his family. It was a story about a great-great-great-grandfather who married into a family with the same eyes.

The year was 1620 when La China Poblana, an Asian woman, came to Pueblo, Mexico as a servant and left her mark on this Spanish Colonial region with her dancing eyes and her colorful fashions.

La China was bought by Miguel de Sosa, who baptized the young girl and gave her a Christian name,

Catarina de San Juan. Catarina married Domingo Suarez, another Chinese servant, confirming the legend that she was Chinese. As well as being a legendary beauty, Catarina became a well-known healer who helped many people. There is a statue in Puebla honoring Catarina for her generosity to others. To pay tribute to her, the women wore her dress style known as China Poblana.

The baby Maria quickly became one of the family. Mrs. Blackly took Arrayo shopping so that Maria would look like all the other children at school. Maria studied hard and was an excellent student. She graduated from high school with honors and a scholarship to the University of Los Angeles, and then went on to medical school when few women were selected to attend. Maria knew she had to take care of her parents who did so much for her, and the only way was to have a good education.

In the meantime Pedro and Arrayo became citizens, making the Blacklys very proud. As they aged, the Blacklys needed more help. Pedro, Arrayo and Maria were asked to move into their large home. They were like one big family and fond of each other. Maria even called Mrs. Blackly "Nana".

Maria opened her private medical practice in Los Angeles where there was a large Mexican population. There she met a Chinese/American physician and soon they married. For their honeymoon, Maria took her parents to Puebla and introduced her husband to the family history of La China Poblana.

Maria and her husband had three children. The two boys looked Asian, but the girl looked more Mexican with an olive color to her skin. Maria lived long enough to see her great grandchildren graduate from college, and to see them follow the tradition of La China Poblana in helping others who were less fortunate.

Our DNA and our genes do not lie. Maria is a great example of how physical traits and even a predisposition towards generosity of spirit can be passed from generation to generation.

HEDDY & ANNABELL

Life sometimes presents us with angels in human form, who change our destiny forever. This story was told to me in 1975 by Mr. Levy, who was dying of cancer. Mr. Levy's wife died some years earlier, and there were only two elderly ladies who devotedly came to visit him each day. Their story follows.

Hedwig and Anna were born in East Prussia, around 1896. That section of Europe had seen many wars, and in the late 1890's was a mix of people, some Russian, Polish, and of course, Prussian German. The latter spoke a High German, and were somewhat regal in their mannerisms.

Their father, Herman, was an educated mining engineer. Their mother, Ida, was a pretty blonde who had a sheltered upbringing in a wealthy family. The father worked for a firm that was investing in mines across the globe. As a result, he made many trips to Cuba to investigate the copper mines there. Herman was a tall, strong, good-looking fellow and also a ladies' man. He had his lovers wherever he traveled. The one he most often visited was a Polish girl who lived in Berlin.

Ida was distraught over the gossip about her husband, which resulted in her having a nervous breakdown. She neglected her three daughters who were ages seven, five, and two. They were dirty, thin and unfed. Ida's family did not live nearby and did not see the entire scene as it played out, or they surely would have helped. When Herman returned from one of his trips to witness his wife talking to herself, and the three girls crying, hungry and dirty, he was beside himself. He placed his wife in a mental institution and the three girls in an orphanage. The wife died within two months, and the oldest girl was so starved she died from an infection.

Hedwig and Anna were left in the orphanage, where they were told about their mother and sister dying. It was a miracle that they survived, but both bore the emotional scars for the rest of their lives.

Herman wanted to escape from the responsibilities of his other family, especially since the Polish girl was pregnant. They waited to go where they could carve out a new life for themselves. They sailed to Cuba where he invested a good deal of money in copper mines, and then sailed to Florida. It was on that trip that the ship's Captain married them. Herman met another German man who was on his way to

Tampa looking for work. Herman said he was going to purchase farmland and would need a manager. A deal was struck. Herman purchased a sugar beet farm with a large house and several other buildings; it was a huge spread. Hugo would manage the land and have a place to hang his hat.

After the house was furnished and farm help hired, it was now in Hugo's hands. Herman left for New York City to find work. He was fortunate to locate a firm looking for a mining engineer who could appraise a mine's value. Herman traveled across the United States and forwarded his findings to the company. This venture yielded excellent results for Herman and the firm.

When Herman arrived back in Florida he had a new baby and when he left for another adventure there was another baby on the way. Back in Germany, Herman's sister, Clara, went to visit the girls in the orphanage. Once the staff at the home heard about the father's new life, he was ordered by the court to take the girls and to pay for the years they had been in the home. Clara and her husband, Claude, decided to sail to America and bring the girls to Florida, then travel to New York City. Clara was a nurse, and had no children, while Claude was a teacher of languages.

They both felt that New York City would afford them the very best opportunity. They took the girls to Florida, and after introducing them to their new family of a brother, sister, and stepmother, they left for New York.

The stepmother used the older girl, Hedwig, as a babysitter and the younger one, Anna, to feed the chickens and gather the eggs. They were not sent to school, with the excuse that they did not speak English. They were not given shoes, toothbrushes or nice clean clothes as they had in the orphanage. They learned English by listening to the farm help. In general, from every viewpoint, they were abused by this wicked woman and made into her slaves.

After four years had passed, Clara and Claude had made a very nice life themselves, and decided to visit her brother in Florida. After Clara witnessed the deliberate neglect of the two girls, she was not only furious, she was irate. She took the parents to court. Clara won the case, and took the girls to New York with her, hoping to change their futures.

Those four years in Florida had left deep emotional scars in the two girls, and Aunt Clara was not known to be a patient soul. She also had a compulsive personality and expected quicker results.

Claude helped the girls with English and both girls became passable students considering the time that was lost. However, both girls inherited their mother's musical talent; they loved to sing and dance with Claude. When the girls reached the ages of eighteen and sixteen, they found jobs sewing in a factory.

With the girls established, Aunt Clara and Claude longed to see their parents in Germany and thought the girls would manage for a few weeks on their own. They sailed off at a peaceful time, but WWII broke out, and they were unable to return to the United States because they were not citizens.

Hedwig and Anna were two blondes who had grown to encompass all the attributes to be movie stars – either could be another Marlene Dietrich if only someone would discover them. Instead of feeling alone and sad, they joined the other girls at the factory, and after work they went dancing with the Army boys. The girls could not afford Aunt Clara's apartment and had to locate to a smaller place. They moved furniture and sold some, because they had no idea when their aunt and uncle would return.

It was during a farewell dance for the soldiers when a man approached the girls. He told them he was in show business and enjoyed watching them dance. He gave them his business card and asked them to place a call for an appointment. The next Saturday they were in an office waiting to see Mr. Levy. Mr. Levy was charming and realized he had two birds in one hand that were lovely to look at as well as talented. They both had dancing legs but they needed a makeover. First their names had to be changed; then they were given a few singing lessons and diction training to make them sound more cultivated.

The girls agreed to work with Mr. Levy on the weekends only, since they had to earn a living and Mr. Levy acquiesced. They could keep their factory jobs until they were ready for a change. Every weekend they had dancing and singing lessons, which were fun. They were naturals in front of a mirror with people watching. The day Mr. Levy said, "I have a show to put you both in – are you ready to quit your factory job?" they both agreed.

The first show they were in was a chorus line. In the second show they were the lead dancers, followed by nightclub acts and other musicals. Mr. Levy was their guardian angel.

One day the two stars asked their manager, "Why are you so nice to us?"

Mr. Levy replied, "Because I understand where you are coming from; and I, too, have had a very sad life." He shared with them his own story:

My parents left Russia around 1880, and sailed to the promise land of peace, America. They had some friends living in lower Manhattan who offered to help them. My father was employed, and my dear mother was pregnant with me. By the time I was three years old my mother was pregnant again, only that time she died in childbirth. It depressed the household, but the loyal friends took care of me along with their children. My father was able to pay our share, and that went on for some time.

One night when my father was walking home, a gang of Irish kids hit him on the head and stole his pay. He died from a hemorrhage. I was about ten years old and took the news of both parents leaving me in a place all alone with unbelievable grief. The kindness of that family pulled me through my darkest days and nights; I will never forget what they did for me. They knew I had my mother's musical ability. When their daughter had a piano lesson, I went along and when we arrived home I practiced the lesson alongside their daughter. By the time I was sixteen, I was playing every tune from Mozart to whatever song

I heard. I finished high school, got a job playing piano at several restaurants, and paid the family for all their help. By the time I was twenty years old, I could support myself and I was on my own.

The young women sympathized with Mr. Levy and they found that they were even more grateful that fate had brought them all together. They couldn't imagine what their future would have been like without him.

One day, news arrived that Aunt Clara and Uncle Claude were killed during one of the bombings. Their ties with the Florida family were severed. Now for the very first time they truly knew what it was like to be on their own. They made Mr. Levy their business manager and officially adopted their new names: Hedwig became Heddy Shaw and Anna became Annabell Shaw. Their German accents were not that noticeable, but considered rather charming and glamorous. After the war years they advanced to more productions, and by the 1930s they were dancing with all the Broadway stars and singing on the radio. There was no stopping their hidden talents and popularity.

The early scars in their lives never affected their careers. But they never loved any one person, they never married, they were never heard to say, "I love you", and they remained friendly, but aloof at all social gatherings. Mr. Levy became more and more aware of this fault in their personalities and asked about their past. The girls trusted him. Once he heard the entire story, he told them this would make a great movie. He introduced them to a writer. The book was a success and was a good seller for many years. All the names and places were changed, of course, to keep their story fiction and to prevent any legal difficulties. A movie followed in 1936 making the girls and Mr. Levy very rich. They were truly movie stars in their own right.

Heddy and Annabell continued to visit Mr. Levy until his death. They never forgot his generosity and kindness to them.

JAKE

Life is a tapestry. Each person in our genealogy makes a thread to create a unique design. When a thread is broken or weakened, the tapestry becomes frayed and loses its design, but sometimes it can be patched up.

This is Jake's story.

California is known for free love, hippies, pop culture and Jesus freaks, all of which made a robust entrance into our society beginning in the 1950s. This was followed by a drug revolution – we were, and still are, in a society out of control.

Jake's mother, Lucy, in her late teens, was caught up in this lifestyle. Lucy had a boyfriend and a drug habit, and soon discovered that she was pregnant. Her son, Jake, was reared in a dysfunctional home and Lucy died from an overdose when the boy was ten years old.

His father, Robert Duncan, became a loyal and devoted parent. Jake adored him, and clung to him. Robert held a job as a baker in a local bread factory. He did his best for the boy but since Jake was known to be a slow learner there wasn't enough money to have him tested. Robert worked with Jake on his schoolwork, but even so Jake could barely pass the exams at the end of each term.

Robert never allowed Jake to curse or use bad language for fear he would fall into a gang. Jake was kept busy doing house chores and working for neighbors. He developed a strong build pushing lawnmowers and grew to be 5' 8" tall, broad-shouldered, with strong arms. In general he was as hard as a rock; but his strong physique belied his learning difficulties.

Jake's father was killed in an auto accident when Jake was eighteen years old. At that age, and with a disability, friends wondered what would become of Jake. The money Jake earned could not pay the rent for the apartment, and eventually Jake was asked to leave the place he called home.

Jake lived on the streets, and became somewhat reclusive after his father died. An old friend of Robert's spotted Jake on the street and after a few friendly words, Jake began to trust him. Old Joe knew of the boy's shortcomings and said, "You do not have to live under a bridge or on the streets. I know just the right place for you. I'll give you the bus fare to Dallas, and you will see my friend for a job."

Jake gathered up the few items he had, placed them in a suitcase, and walked to the bus depot. The disheveled teenager purchased a ticket to Dallas, and set his heart on a new adventure and a new life.

The address Joe gave him led him to a small storefront in downtown Dallas. The name on the door read, 'Rodeo Performances: Felix Underwood.' A kindly middle-aged man sat behind the desk. Jake said, "Joe sent me for a job." The moment Felix glanced at Jake's strong frame he remarked, "Good, I'll teach you to ride a horse like your rear-end is glued to its back. It's a ride without control to sit on a wild beast, to be carried along with such speed by something so wild and kicking and bucking." The more the man talked, the more aware Jake became of the dangers of being a bronco rider. This wasn't at all what he expected.

Felix said, "Each time you ride for me, you will be paid, and if you are really good, I'll enter you into different events around the states. My crew will take care of you. If you have any problems, you come to me. I will always be around when you ride. But first you have to learn how to break in horses at my ranch for one year. That will give you the training and understanding of a horse's temperament."

When Jake heard about the money and being taken care of, he was determined to be a bronco rider, and a good one. Jake said, "Wham bam I am in a jam!" This was one of Jake's favorite sayings.

Felix held out his hand and said, "Joe, your father's friend, phoned me to assure me you were a reliable person and we should place our confidence in each other. Let us shake and start a lasting friendship with good luck for both of us."

"If you teach me, I'll perform for you Mr. Underwood, and I'll survive. I promise," he said. "Thank you."

After one year on the ranch in New Mexico learning how to break in horses, Jake learned how to control a horse. Jake had a special way of talking into a horse's ear; it was his special touch and along with a pat on its head, that seemed to calm the uncontrollable beasts. Felix made the trip to New Mexico to watch Jake's progress. Then that day came when Felix put Jake on a horse that was a little rough, but nothing compared to what he would later be sitting on. Jake started to talk to the horse as if the dumb animal was the only company he needed. Jake soon discovered that he had a calming effect on each horse Felix put him on.

Felix brought out the fourth horse for Jake to hold onto and said a little prayer as he told Jake to work his charm. Jake patted the rough beast, mounted, and started to whisper in its ear. It was astonishing to see the serenity of the horse and how Jake sat firmly in place and held on for dear life. Felix told his boys, "I think we have a winner. Our next stop will be Fort Worth." It was a day's workout for Jake, and by this time he looked like yesterday's Danish with the puff collapsing. Felix said, "You did a great job for a kid who never rode before; you keep it up and we will be winners."

Through the years Jake stayed with Felix and Company, there were more human-interest stories in the papers and on television about Jake's ability to ride in competitions and to win. Finally, in Fort Worth's big bronco event, Jake was given a horse to ride that was known to throw the best rider.

After six years of Jake's riding, the moment of truth was before Felix's eyes, a horse named Greased Lightening. It was just one of those days when Felix wanted to throw his hands up and say every curse word he knew, but instead he went over to Jake to breathe in confidence to every cell in Jake's body. "You can do it, show them," he told him.

"Wham, bam, I'm in a jam!" Jake replied.

Greased Lightening was brought into the pen. Jake mounted, holding the reins with all his strength. Before the gate opened, Jake patted the horse on its head the same way he did with all the others and leaned forward to whisper in its ear, which always seemed to be a magical touch, but not this time. The moment the gates opened Jake's hat blew off, and he bounced around on that beast, going in circles, all around the corral – but Jake held onto the beast. The last curve was almost Jake's death ride – the beast went so close to the wall that the people in the stands had to scramble. Felix said in a muffled voice, "Either that horse or rider will be crippled or deformed."

Jake held on for dear life. It was, indeed, the ride of his life. The horse, like its name, had thrown its body against the wall several times causing its hindquarters to bleed. Jake's leg had taken a beating too. The eight minutes were up. The bell rang and the spectators roared. Felix hugged Jake and said, "You won the Big One, kid."

Jake was awarded a very large silver and gold buckle with an embossed horse that very few riders achieve, plus $25,000 prize money. Kind-hearted Jake made a large contribution to the homeless shelter in

Fort Worth, and felt his dream was completed. For many years Jake worked on Felix's ranch breaking in horses and training future bronco riders. But Jake was never seen without wearing that silver buckle. If the sunbeams shone on that buckle it would almost seem as though that horse was bucking up a storm.

Jake suffered with leg pain for many years after that. He always had a soft spot for all injured riders. He made his rounds in the different hospitals to visit them and give them hope. Many had suffered head injuries and spinal problems.

At the age of sixty, Jake found himself in the hospital having his leg x-rayed because it was more painful and he could barely walk. The doctor told him the bones had split and would need an operation to have rods put inside. The surgery was successful, but Jake had a rough ride ahead; it was many weeks of physical therapy and a slow recovery.

Through the years, Jake had gained too much weight and was diabetic. This caused Jake to make a special belt so that he could proudly wear his special buckle high around his waist, and tell his story to anyone who inquired or showed the slightest interest.

I was one of those who asked about the beautiful belt buckle. Jake's story also reminds me that personal success is not necessarily measured by our possessions or our intellectual achievements, but by how well we love others.

LOVE, LOSS
&
LETTING GO

AUSSIE

Perhaps the most unusual and romantic request I ever received was from a man in his late 70's.

When I met Aussie in Kentucky in 2010, he was a still a very handsome and intelligent person and fun to know. His wife was in a nursing home, suffering from Alzheimer's disease and Aussie was in the hospital recovering from a car accident where he had broken both knees, his wrist and fingers.

"It's so sad," Aussie told me. "My wife doesn't recognize the children or me anymore. We keep visiting and sit with her for hours, hoping for a breakthrough. But now I can't even go to see her."

"Is there anything I can do for you?" I asked.

"Yes," he replied. "Write a love letter for me, please."

"Okay. On one condition," I told him. "That you tell me all about growing up in Kentucky. Deal?"

"Deal."

Here is what Aussie told me.

I was born in 1932 in the mountains of eastern Kentucky, the last of nine children born to parents who could not help us with our schoolwork. In spite of that they were intelligent people. My mother was just fifteen years old when she married, too young to rear a family and be a good manager, but we got by.

Let me tell you about our names. Daddy named us after countries and cities that he heard people talk about when he was young. My name is Aussie for (Australia), and then there is Lexie (Lexington), Athena (Greece), Callie (California), Virginia (for the state), Fran (France), Roma (Rome), Oslo (Norway) and Genoa (Italy).

The Depression years were hard on folks like us. We lived in a one-room house that was more like a shack, with no running water or electricity. We did not know we were poor folks, because everyone around us was poor, too. We made our own fun growing up. We picked berries, chestnuts, edible seeds and roots. Daddy would hunt and fish, and Mama would plant a vegetable garden. It was sheer luck and lots of praying that got us through one year after another.

We young'uns were given baptisms in a creek by the preacher. Baptisms took place every summer and the entire town turned out for the event and a picnic afterwards. Another thing I remember was hunting and fishing with my Dad and how Mama cooked every bit of the kill. Also I recall how the girls helped on laundry day, placing all the washed laundry on tall shrubs or tree branches to dry. Most of all I remember the beauty of those mountains that surrounded us and the wild flowers that grew everywhere.

When I was about twelve years old my Daddy thought I had a keen brain and deserved a better life. I was very well behaved and one of his favorites. On one of his hunting trips he met a doctor who inquired if he knew anyone who could help with his four boys. That was the day my life changed. Helping the boys with their schoolwork was fun. My new life in a small town was fun, having my own bed was fun, eating different foods was fun, having meals served with silver pieces on the table was fun. I was having the time of my life and going to school with the doctor's children.

I finished high school in 1950. The four boys were doing well in school and my services were no longer needed. Industry was coming into Kentucky and I found an excellent position and attended college at night. I fell head-over-heels in love with another student and we married right after graduation. We had four children. Life was good, we purchased a house, and in time the children went off to college, the military or got married. We were good parents, loving one another, doing the right thing and going to church — that was our lives.

Now old age has caught up with us. You would be an angel to write a love letter to my wife. One extra favor — could you please write it four times? That way each week I can mail her a letter. It would mean the world to me.

How could I refuse Aussie? Still love-struck and yearning for his lovely bride, he remains the most incurable romantic I have ever met.

JOHN

Sometimes real love means learning to let go. John Burns, age seventy-five, was once a person with a huge, strong body, a dynamic countenance and slicked-down grey hair. He never had any visitors, which seemed terribly odd since he had four living children. Therefore; whenever I could, I tried to extend my visits with him to listen to his stories.

John Burns' paternal grandmother, Ida, and his paternal grandfather, Henry, were both Scotch-Irish. Both were born in the United States and for one reason or another they settled in northern Kentucky.

These Irish grandparents were John's favorite and the ones he knew the best. Grandpa Gordon owned a chain of hardware stores, which afforded young John all the tools, nails, and wood to build things. It was not long before his talents were recognized, for this boy could dream up weird shapes with movable parts. One day Grandpa Gordon told him, "You are not cut out for academics, but to work with your hands." Those words stayed in his memory bank and were cherished by John. His Grandma Gordon was a wonderful cook and baked him his favorite treats, all of which may account for John's large build and his love for good food.

John's maternal grandmother and grandfather were full blooded-Cherokee Indians who lived their lives in Central Kentucky. The maternal grandparents were somewhat different in temperament and also in appearance. Since Kentucky had a fairly large population of Cherokee Indians from the early years in history, these facts were not disturbing but were accepted with great tolerance. By this time in history the Cherokee people were educated, lived in nice homes that were furnished with all the modern interiors. They owned farms, cattle, and had their own businesses. However, all through the early history of their tribal people, they were mistreated and fought in wars. It was not a pleasant history for the Cherokee people, especially when they were a friendly tribal group with the early settlers, and the fact that the U.S. government did not honor their treaties or their land rights.

With these factors in mind, and the stories that were told from one generation to the next; it was no wonder that an undercurrent of animosity towards those who were British or French still existed. The Cherokees had their own little communities. Some married outside the tribe, but many stayed and remained full-blooded Cherokee.

Rosie was John's maternal grandparents' first-born, and she grew up into a tall, thin beauty by anyone's standards. Rosie was sent to schools and had a head for business.

John's father, Paul, had a somewhat privileged life and always felt that he could do as he pleased. He was educated through high school, and then worked in the hardware stores owned by Grandpa Gordon. It was his temperament that caused too many problems, and his father told him to find work elsewhere. In Irish culture it would be termed as having a thick head or very stubborn. When Paul grew into manhood and married the Indian beauty, Rosie, it came as no surprise to his family.

Rosie came into their marriage with dreams of owning a house in the country where she could tend to her garden. The marriage proved to be a nightmare, and as the years passed with disappointment, she became jaded. The marriage showed signs of trouble from the beginning; mainly due to all those nights when Paul drank himself into a stormy tempestuous human being. Six children were born and reared into a dysfunctional household. Paul's inability to get along with people caused the family to move to wherever he could find work. In time, Rosie was abused by her husband, which caused her to be bitter and intolerant toward the boys. If their chores were not finished, the two older boys were beaten daily with a stick or a board.

When he was twelve years old, John and his older brother ran away from the home. They found odd jobs doing yard work. One day a traveling carnival passed through town. They joined the group and these workers became their new family. They were never beaten again. Since both boys were tall and well built, they added a few years to their ages and nobody questioned them.

John stayed with the group for six years during which he learned a number of mechanical chores, which required a lot of skill to assure the carnival rider customers their safety. His brother left the carnival after four years to find work in the coalmines of eastern Kentucky. By the time John was seventeen or eighteen years old he was 6 '2" tall and 200 pounds with a muscle-man body. The men at the carnival gave him the nickname "Mister Testosterone." John was beginning to think he could fulfill a woman's deepest desires. He started to date a pretty girl, Rita, who was employed as a cashier and bookkeeper.

Rita was born in New York City. Her parents came from Puerto Rico. They were hard workers and decent law-abiding citizens. When she was twenty-two, Rita married and had twin boys. The father of Rita's boys was not so responsible. He skipped out on his responsibilities and never was seen again.

John found the babies adorable, and fell head-over-heels in love with Rita. By the time John was nineteen, he married Rita and adopted the twins. Fatherhood was a frightening adventure to embrace. John's parents each gave him important gifts: from his mother he learned not to use his temper, and from his father he was taught not to get drunk, but to work hard at every job.

The thought of leaving the carnival to settle down in one place was not an easy decision, but it had to be done to have a happy family life. It was not long before they purchased a house and John found a position as a welder. Life was not a bowl of cherries at times — it was hard to accept life on its own terms. To John, marriage was a picture of agony and ecstasy. It could be good, but not perfect. With those thoughts in mind, John and Rita stayed together for twenty years.

They had a total of eight children, including another set of twins who died during childbirth, and two who died in a car accident.

Whenever the carnival came to town, John would take his children to meet old friends and to have fun on the rides. His old nickname had more meaning now that he had eight children; and the men remarked, "You must have thought you were an incredible mechanic in the boudoir!"

Rita felt as though she did her very best in managing the household; but there was always that feeling of emptiness. Rita wanted to get a college education and certainly did not want any more children. A short time after celebrating their twentieth wedding anniversary, Rita announced she was leaving for New York City. Rather than watch her grow bitter; they decided to divorce.

The children were teenagers and John agreed to keep them. Rita left home and never returned. This was a surprise to all who knew them because they were kind and loving to each other.

I usually do not ask questions when stories are told to me, but I was curious to finally ask a few. I wondered why Rita left and did not return.

John answered with tears in his eyes.

Rita's twin boys were getting ready to go off to Vanderbilt University in Tennessee. I had to work and Rita said she would drive them — it was not that far. The boys sat in the back seat reading when a truck plowed into the rear end of the car. Rita was bruised and had a broken arm, but both boys were killed. Rita never did recover from the shock. The twin boys were the brightest of all the children and we both had high hopes for their futures. They were excellent students. Both were in sports, on the debating team, plus they were handsome boys. It devastated both of us.

Rita needed to be her own person after giving so much time to all the children. I fully understood this and certainly wanted her to be happy. Don't misunderstand me, Rita loved all her children and somehow knew she would see them again when the time was right. Returning home to Kentucky would only bring back all those sweet and bittersweet memories, which would have depressed her. We needed a clean break to survive.

I asked him how Rita managed to support herself and go to college. He explained that the accident was the fault of a trucking company. An out-of-court settlement was agreed upon, which Rita used wisely. Rita lived in the city, not too far from her parents, and studied at New York University. She earned her masters degree in Education and was employed in a high school.

Her four children planned a surprise birthday/graduation party for her at a downtown restaurant where once again they were united with their mother. There were many more reunions with new in-laws and grandchildren. Rita never did return to Kentucky; it remained a clean break with no ties. John was a young forty-year-old man and still good looking. Somehow Rita knew he would find happiness once again.

Most of all I wondered how he managed with four children after Rita left.

I had to find a part-time job as a security guard and I had a housekeeper come in three times a week to help out with the chores. The day was drawing near when the children were ready to leave for college, marriage, or find a job; and then I could sit back and relax.

When that day finally came, and the house was empty of laughter, noise in the kitchen, and fighting in the bedrooms, I nearly lost it with the loneliness and quiet. I took the family to celebrate Christmas and their grandparents' birthdays. However, I went alone to my father's funeral. That was when I decided to move to be closer to my mother since she was losing her memory.

I found another welding job and moved into a small apartment. My beautiful mother never lost her figure or beauty, but she did lose her bitterness and was rather pleasant to be around. She developed brain cancer. Of all the children she had, I was the one who took care of her to the very end.

I was forty-two years old when I was introduced to a woman who was working in the office where I was employed. June was divorced without children, a very sweet thirty-four-year-old person. We dated for three months and married. June said her clock was ticking and she really would love to have at least two children. I agreed and had to pop a Valium to recover after I said yes.

The two children were adorable, but spoiled brats. June's parents doted on the babies since they were the only grandchildren. They gave the children anything and everything through the years. I felt that I no longer had control in my own household. They were not like my other children, who were good students and well mannered.

I stayed in that unhappy marriage sixteen years. One night there was an argument over a car for the boys; and I said, "That's it!" I packed my bags and left. I did support the children until they turned eighteen. I regret to admit this, but we were never close. I worked hard and had no tolerance for spoiled, lazy children.

I divorced June but we remained friends for the children's benefit. As the years passed I did not see much of the two children. Today, they are married and have their own families. At fifty-five, I was still in middle age, and had a good job as a welder. I saved some money and traveled. It was time to enjoy life — my life — my freedom. I visited my brother and sisters at different holidays. I always celebrated Christmas with my four children when it was convenient to have a family gathering.

The years rolled by, and I lived in a senior citizen complex for years until I became ill. Now I am here, talking with you about my life's story — facts I have never told anyone before. It was comforting to tell you. Would you do me one big favor?

I know my time is near; but I would like you to say a prayer with me. My favorite is Psalms 23:

The Lord is my Shepherd; I shall not want.

He maketh me to lie down in green pastures:

He leadeth me beside the still waters.

He restoreth my soul:

He leadeth me in the paths of righteousness

for His name's sake.

Yea, though I walk through the valley

of the shadow of death, I will fear no evil:

For thou art with me;

Thy rod and thy staff, they comfort me.

Thou preparest a table before me

in the presence of mine enemies;

Thou annointest my head with oil;

My cup runneth over.

Surely goodness and mercy shall follow me

all the days of my life,

and I will dwell in the House of the Lord forever.

- King James Version

After we prayed, John closed his eyes and fell asleep. The next time I visited the home; I was told that John passed away with his four children at his side. The other two children sent their condolences but never showed up at the funeral.

ROLAND

Roland Young resembled a forest tree in Kentucky — straight, sturdy, strong and solid. But it was when he smiled that the full picture of his personality showed through — his sparkly blue-grey eyes lit up his face and the birds began to sing. I admit this is a fanciful description, but it was what I saw when I first met him in Kentucky in 2010.

I liked Roland and we became friends for a few months. During this time only one or two of his eighteen children were said to visit him. Until one day . . .

I really did not suspect how ill Roland Young was, because he sat tall and erect with all his seventy years in the chair next to mine. Before he could start to talk, the room began to fill up with people of all different ages. I looked at him and said, "Perhaps I should come back."

"   No," he said. "You stay put in that chair."

I counted eighteen people with their mates in the room, totaling thirty-six; and also about twenty-five others, which would have been their children. Now the room was bursting at the seams with sixty people, more or less. A fire regulation was not heeded to be sure.

It was a pastiche of characters. Some were dressed to bow before the Queen, some were in sporty clothes, and some were just plain dirty.

There were no kisses or hugs for the man with blue-grey eyes that suddenly turned angry.

One young man said, "Dad, your doctor phoned to tell us that you refused any further treatment, is that true?"

"Yes, and I am writing my will."

"Dad, I am your first born, the one you taught the construction business to."

"Just a minute," said another. "We are the kids from your second wife, don't we count?"

"Hey you, we are from wife number three."

"Go to hell, we are from number four."

"Forget that, we are from number five."

"Grandpa, I want to go to college," said a young grandson.

"So do I," replied another.

The noise was overwhelming, and this group was turning on one another with words not fit to write down.

Suddenly, Roland rose up from his chair and like a tornado waved his arms for them to shut up.

He turned to look at me and said, "This should be interesting."

"Nobody came to visit me when I was home, because if number two or three kids were there you would not be in the same room with them. Do you kids remember that? Do you kids think I did not support you, and give you every opportunity? College, cars, and weddings — you all got the works. I do not remember ever receiving a thank you note or card. Do any of you remember writing one or even going to a store to buy me a gift?"

You could have heard a pin drop. After that remark, Roland said, "Consider this my funeral with every one of you kids and grandkids here to say goodbye. Well, goodbye, I always loved all of you, and did my very best to help each one of you. I loved your mothers until we had disagreements and went our own ways. That is all I have to say, now please just leave."

Heads were hung low in embarrassment, and one by one they left the room without a kiss or goodbye hug for their father.

After they all left, Roland said, "I want to write a will. I understand you are a notary. As you can see, I am of mixed race – black, white and Cherokee. There are too many veterans from these Mid-Eastern wars, and I would like to set up a foundation to help the wounded and veterans when they are older and in a nursing home and to help their children go to college. This would be the best way to help all races, and those who fought for this country, and let them know they are not forgotten." Your job is to locate an attorney who can set up the foundation for which you will be paid for your time. In the meantime I must write a will."

Here is what Roland dictated:

This is my last will and testimony as dictated. I bequeath all my savings and the Young Construction Company to a Roland Young Foundation. The construction company can be sold to the U.S. Government or a private company for no less than $4,000,000.00, which is a fair price. I appoint this attorney and the Veterans of Foreign Affairs to be just and fair in the distribution of all funds.

Signed on this date — 2010 in my own hand and notarized, Roland Young.

The above was carried out as Roland wished. He was cremated and there was no service to attend. His ashes were scattered at a veterans' cemetery by his attorney and myself. His fortune was a billion dollars or more and will benefit those he cared about, who had so little. He left nothing to his ungrateful children or grandchildren.

MARGIE

It is never too late to express our love to your family. When I met Margie, she was very sad. She had just received news that she would never live long enough to see her granddaughter.

"A letter is always something she can keep to remember you. Let us write a clever letter from your heart," I suggested.

"That sounds great!" she agreed. This is what she wrote:

Dear Sweet Allison,

I thank you for the lovely photos and hearing your sweet voice over the telephone. I pray each night that your mommy and daddy will come home safe and sound from Iraq to watch you grow up. Your Grandma on the West Coast is having all the fun, and here I am on the East Coast wishing I could hold you and just look at you.

I would love to hear you say: "Why is your hair two different colors? Why is your skin so wrinkly, crinkly? Why, Granny, did you forget to do that?" Why, why, and why?"

I miss not having crumbs on the floor after each meal, or no cookies on the chairs, or never having flour all over the floor, or fingerprints to wash off the walls, and I never, never hear myself saying, "No!" a thousand times. I miss not hearing a giggle. I miss not making a mess baking cookies. I miss not having the pleasure of reading a book to you, or teaching you a new word. I miss not giving hugs and kisses to you.

I have watched you grow up through snap-shots. I have wondered about your measurements when I purchase clothes for you. I am amazed when I hear your voice over the telephone. I wish you were not so far away. I would love to hold your hand and take a walk, or go to the zoo, or have a tea party, or just to read a book with you.

I guess this will have to wait, but know that I love you and miss you with all my heart.

Your loving Granny Ward

Margie Ward died from cancer of the liver in 2008. She mailed her letter, but sadly was never able to meet her granddaughter Allison in person.

WISDOM

&

GRATITUDE

EMMA

One of the most generous and self-aware people I have ever known was Emma. When I met her in 1983, she asked me to help her write an article for a newspaper or magazine about her life story.

I was curious. "Why have you waited all these years to write something, surely you could have written it before now?" I asked her.

"I really did not know or realize the damage my behavior could cause, nor did I know the reason behind such actions until recently," she replied. Here is the very intimate, but tragic story Emma told me.

My parents came from England, where they both had a very strict upbringing. They came to the United States as young children before WWI. Both were highly educated. They met at MIT, where they were obtaining their engineering degrees, and they later had a successful business.

I was their only child, and reared under the doctrine, 'children should be seen and not heard' — more or less the same way they were reared.

Now I ponder why Hitler and North Korea or other militaristic countries can have such control over the youth. Could it be that the youth were always told what to do, and could not express themselves?

My mother was obsessed with work and success, and not the usual stay-at-home mother. It probably was a good thing that she did not want to waste her education staying at home.

I was placed in excellent boarding schools, and came home on the usual holidays. I, too, became well educated and earned an MBA and had several excellent positions before I landed in Washington D.C. working for a large government-owned firm. Up until Washington D.C. fever set in, I lived with my parents in New York City. Now I was completely on my own to make my own decisions. In other words, I finally felt free and wanted to experience everything new and different.

I always had a flair for nice clothes and certainly with my blonde hair, blue eyes, slim figure, brains, and all the other attributes, was the talk among men. When I went out on a date with the same fellow more than once, it always ended up in bed. Now I realize that I was looking for love, not a one-night stand. I had two abortions done on the sly – several infections – and now cancer, which will cause my death. After years of analysis to cope with my depression, I realized why I never found Mr. Right to love me. My promiscuous behavior all led me to where I am today.

A person can be educated, have a great career, be beautiful or handsome; but if you have never felt loved as a child, and then as an adult you go looking for it, you are most certainly looking for trouble. All children need both parents to guide them through life's journey. My parents were too busy with their own lives to have a child.

Children need both parents regardless if they are rich or poor; they need guidance and wisdom that can only come from parents — not a school, books, a position or money. Boys who join a gang are looking for that father figure they never had. Girls who have loose behavior patterns are in need of a mother's guidance, not one who is a druggie or one obsessed with her career. Today there are AIDs and other diseases that are very costly, not only in a monetary sense, but worst of all in relationships.

My parents have died and here I am with a wonderful inheritance and my own savings at age sixty-five, with not a person who cares whether I live or die. If I had one wish, it would be for every child to live feeling good about him or herself and to have the feeling of being loved.

Before she died, the story Emma shared with me was published in several magazines and newspapers as she wished. But I have never forgotten how she came to understand herself late in life. Emma left her entire inheritance to cancer research.

FRANCESCA

One of the most gripping stories related to me was that of a horrible crime committed during WWII.

In 2009, Francesca still had her Polish accent, still had a beautiful face, still had her ingenious character, and still had all the scars of that war. Francesca sat in the bed with both legs on pillows. She was eighty-six years old, and in much pain physically and mentally. I asked her if I could do anything for her — write letters, read to her — but she always replied, "There is no one left to write to."

"Oh, you don't mean that," I said.

"Yes I do," replied Francesca. "They are all gone. My family, mother, father, grandparents, a younger and older sister are all gone."

"How did that happen?" I asked. Here is Francesca's story.

One day they took all the Jewish people and loaded us on the back of an open truck and drove to a camp. We were told to get out. They separated my family; only my older sister and I were in one line and the rest of the family was in another line. My sister and I were put in a large room where we waited and waited with all the others. After all these hours of travel and waiting, we were all hungry. The odor that greeted us smelled like soup being served; the smell of homemade soup was making all of us anxious. It was only later that we found out that the scent came from the ovens burning bodies, and of course there never was any soup.

I never saw my family again. My sister developed the flu and died in my arms as we sat on a cold, damp floor. Every morning and night I had to march five miles to and from a factory to make bullets for Hitler's war. The second winter my legs were badly frostbitten and turning blue with deep holes, making it impossible for me to walk that distance. I was sent to a German doctor who saved my life. He gave me a cream and bandages and left orders that I could not march until the holes were healed. He truly saved my life, such as it was.

At the end of the war, I went back to our house where my father had buried his most valuable items. A long-time neighbor had joined him in burying his own valuables there. I approached that tree in the backyard, only to find that our neighbor must have gotten to it first. I had nothing, just rags on my back.

There were agencies to help us, and in time I found my way to New York City. It was through a synagogue that I found a family to live with, and employment in a factory. One day I was walking to work and a young man stopped me to ask directions.

It was a joke, since we were both considered to be greenhorns with thick Jewish accents. After talking with him, we discovered our camps in Warsaw were next to each other and that he was living with another family just a few doors down the same street I was living on. It really is a small world.

We saw each other every day, and in time we married. He had lost his family, too, and we found comfort in each other. My dear, sweet husband died five years ago. Now you know why I am alone with no letters to write. Everyone is dead.

"I am so sorry, Francesca, that you had to suffer at such a young age and like so many other people," I expressed to her.

"I wish we could go back in time to change it," Francesca replied.

"Believe me, we would if we could," I agreed. "Many lives were lost at the hands of sinister people. So many people are in their graves, and no one will ever know the thwarted hopes and dreams of their lives. But you did have a life, and you found love and compassion to share with someone who understood what it was like; and for that I am grateful."

We all have personal crises, but this story still jars every bone in my body. Francesca died from infections and diabetes shortly after telling me her story. I can only imagine how many more stories like this have never been revealed.

LITTLE TREE

By nature we tend to guard our privacy, to hold onto our former lives in order to hold onto memories whether they be good ones, bad ones or those filled with lies. Today I was asked to write a letter for a patient. She spoke so softly and was so difficult to understand, that nobody wanted to assist her with even one letter.

What a shame! Her story is a fascinating one.

When I walked into the room, my eyes fell upon a small bundle in the bed. When she pulled down the sheet, she revealed one of the most sun-damaged faces I have ever seen. Clearly, this woman had worked hard in her life. Her skin was the color of dried up mud cakes, lined and cracked and ready to break up. The lips caused her mouth to create deeply etched lines on each side. The hair was like a flying cloud of white cotton fluff, with some tied into a long braid. The eyes that looked intently back at you were coal black and so fiery that they could burn holes in the blanket. But the most interesting feature was her high cheekbones. I took a deep breath and said, "I am here to write a letter for you. Shall we start?"

Her lips shifted in bewilderment and little rivers of tears started to run down her cheeks. Then she started to talk in that soft elegant voice, which did not fit her appearance. Here is what she dictated to me:

November 20, 1988
Dear Son,

I know it was your eighty-sixth birthday, and that you had several strokes and cannot write or phone anymore. There are a few things you should know before I go that I have never told anyone before; and I do mean no one.

It was on a Saturday, September 8, 1900, that a hurricane swept across West Texas. As a result of that terrible storm, St. Mary's Orphanage that was part of Galveston Island, now sat on the ocean floor, taking ninety innocent children to their deaths. There were 35,000 homes gone, which fell apart brick by brick and sank to the bottom, never to be seen again. There were so many dead bodies that they burned them on the beach. It was one of the greatest tragedies in American history.

I could have been one of those children because I had lived in that orphanage since I was three months old. All I was told about my parents was that both were Comanche Indians and they could not care for me. Both were very ill with a fever and died shortly after I was brought to St. Mary's.

On that fateful morning in September, I was selected to go with Sister Lucille, who was maybe sixty years old, to pick up some supplies on the mainland. We left late in the afternoon. Sister Lucille tucked a box with some money under her seat and we had a lunch basket in the back of the wagon. Then we were off. What a treat that was for me to travel out of the orphanage! We crossed over on the bridge. The winds were getting stronger, and things just did not look normal. We stopped and we learned about the hurricane hitting the island. The wind picked up, spooking the horses. They reared and just at that moment, Sister Lucille must have had a heart attack. She slumped over in the seat. Luckily, a priest was nearby. He helped me bring Sister Lucille to the church and he promised to take care of her until my return.

Nobody asked me any questions, people were running around wildly and things were flying through the air. It simply was not safe to just stay there. I was so frightened and worried about Sister Lucille, but I stayed calm; she had taught me well how to drive the wagon and hold onto the horses. I just jumped into the seat and headed northwest where the sky was a little clearer. As I looked around at the wide-open spaces, I said to myself, "I am free as a bird and the winds carried me here for a new life. Little Tree, spread your branches and reach for the sky."

Finally, I came upon a small town. While the horses were fed at a livery, I decided to rest close by and eat the food that was in the basket. A small boy wandered over to me. He looked hungry so I offered him a sandwich. He appeared to be about five or six years old. His name was James. James told me his father was waiting for his wagon to be repaired.

It was not long before a weary gentleman approached me. He thanked me for feeding his son, and I offered the third sandwich to him. He ate it with much gusto, which made me think they were in trouble. He asked me what my plans were out in this open country by myself. I lied and told him my parents died and I was looking for work. He told me his wife died, and he was going north to work on a cotton farm. He told me that his wagon was in bad shape and did not know how he could reach his destination.

I did not know where I was or where I was going. Since the Sisters at the orphanage had educated me, I was smart enough to seize the opportunity and said, "This was an act by God that we should meet like this." Looking him in the eye I asked him if he believed in God. The answer was "Yes, by all means, we always went to Church every Sunday and prayed before we ate our evening meal."

"Well, mister, that is good enough for me and you both can travel with me."

Son, that is how I met your father, Jonas Martin, who was the nicest man any girl could wish for.

Bad news travels fast, and it was not long before we heard about that disaster that hit Galveston Island. I never told him I was from the orphanage, and he only asked me my name and age. I told another lie and said my name was Easter Wood, when my real name was Little Tree. My age was fifteen, and I had schooling enough to find a job in a store or some business. Easter was always my favorite holiday and that is why I chose it for my name. It was a new start on my life's journey.

After Jonas Martin sold his wagon and horses and placed the few packages in my wagon, we were headed north.

Your father was a proper man. He caught fish and cooked the meals we ate on the trip north. We slept on the roadside. I told him the clothes I had in the wagon were stolen. After much conversation, we decided to marry at a church in a small town. It took us about three weeks with several stops and tending to James.

Your father came from Louisiana and had some high school. His father could not pay his bills and they traveled to Texas to start over. It was a hard life and his wife died in childbirth, leaving him with Jonas to settle down. Nothing was easy. Jonas was accustomed to all the knock-me-downs and get-up-agains in life. Now here he was living his father's life all over again.

We managed with the money Sister Lucille had in that box. I always wondered how many supplies we were to bring back. It haunts me to this day that I left Sister Lucille behind. I pray for her soul, and that I will be forgiven.

After days of traveling, we settled in a small town, which was considered West Texas. Jonas managed to be a hired hand on a cotton farm, and later worked in the cotton gin during harvest time. He was fortunate to be given a small house near the farm, with terms that he was to make the repairs if we decided to stay. We leaped with joy, and I found work at the General Mercantile Store. I taught Jonas in the evenings and enrolled him a local school. It was a year later that you were born.

We both loved you, even though you thought I pushed you aside. We were very busy people and life was not easy. I helped to pull cotton and dragged you on my back across the cotton fields. James had his mother, who was a dear person who loved him so he knew love and could return it. I never had a mother or father to show me love, and maybe that is why it was so difficult for me to even say the words, "I love you Sonny." But, please know, even at this late date in both of our lives, that I always loved you. It was all those early years of hard work picking cotton that we were able to purchase 5,000 acres of land and have a more comfortable life.

I am so very proud that you became the man you are — sweet, soft spoken, educated, well-liked by everyone. You had a wonderful wife and children, traveled all over the world, fought for your country, and served in the military for thirty years. You cannot imagine how proud we were when you graduated from West Point in the top ten of your class, and all those years you worked in Washington, D.C.

Sonny, please know I have always loved your family, and I want you to know how proud your father was of you. I recently signed all the mineral rights on the farmland over to your children, and to your brother James' two sons. I realize this could have been done years earlier, but the grandchildren would have been spoiled rotten. The farmland was sold for your children to be educated and afford them a good life.

I guess living a long life makes one tough and yields wisdom that nobody wants. That's my story, which may answer some questions in your mind.

I love you and wish we had not been separated by miles through all these years.

All my love,

Mother Little Tree, Easter Martin

Easter Martin did not live long after this letter was mailed to her son. I will never forget the smile on her face when I placed the letter in the envelope. It was the last chapter in one of the most interesting stories I have ever encountered.

RALPH

In 1995 I had the occasion to spend time with Ralph, a twelve-year-old boy in hospice care. Needless to say it broke my heart that he was going to die so soon. Despite this, Ralph always had a sunny disposition and a big smile on his face when I came to see him.

Ralph didn't want me to read to him, he just wanted answers. Surprisingly, he did not want to know about his cancer; but wondered about many things, including what happens when a person dies. Here is what Ralph told me one day.

I have a Bucket List for Space and God. I hope when I die, I can step out onto those white puffy clouds in space. When I do, here is what I'd like.

1. I want to see men living on the moon.

2. I want to see space ships and know which planet they are from.

3. I want to be able to solve the mystery about which planet has a civilized society, and whether they started the civilization on Earth.

4. I want to know how those people live on their planet, and do they have wars and kill each other or do they live peacefully.

5. I want to talk to Michelangelo, Schopenhauer, Newton, Nietzsche, Shakespeare, Milton, Keats, Jack London, Walt Disney, and all the movie stars who gave me hours of pleasure.

6. I want to look down on Earth and see happy people who are not killing each other.

7. I want to see God on his throne and ask him why we have wars instead of peace, and why do people commit crimes and kill each other.

8. I want to ask God to change the people on earth.

9. I want God to unite all religions.

10. I want to thank God for my life and all the blessings he has bestowed on me.

I realized that only God could answer Ralph's questions and grant his dreams. I was very profoundly impressed by the depth of this young man's need to know and by his humanitarian view of the world.

ABOUT THE AUTHOR

Charlotte Cooper has always had the soul of an artist. Born in 1926 on Long Island, New York, she graduated from Taphagen School of Fashion, working for eighteen years as a professional clothing designer. From the beginning, she was also an avid reader and writer, penning her own ad copy whenever her original designs appeared in print.

She married a physician and had two sons. In the early days of their marriage, her husband was in the military and they traveled extensively. She often volunteered in hospitals and nursing homes, meeting people from many different walks of life.

Later, Charlotte's talents turned towards writing and publishing short stories. When she was faced with cancer, and spent time in the hospital herself, she found that people naturally opened up to her. They began to tell her things that they had never shared with anyone before and she realized the therapeutic value of story.

This book is the result of her ability to listen with a compassionate heart and to translate these tales of our human triumphs and sufferings at the end of life. She continues to write, make art and enjoy life in her home in Lexington, Kentucky.

*Azalea Art Press
specializes in visionary novels,
creative fiction & nonfiction, poetry, memoir
& imaginative children's titles.*

To learn more, visit:

http://azaleaartpress.blogspot.com
azalea.art.press@gmail.com

Karen Mireau
Publisher
AZALEA ART PRESS
Berkeley . California

To order more books:
http://www.lulu.com/shop/charlotte-
cooper/exit-path/paperback/product-
20106834.html

www.ingramcontent.com/pod-product-compliance
Lightning Source LLC
Chambersburg PA
CBHW050759250626
47155CB00005B/2140